For Lynn and Kate and Joe—B.C.

To Mike/Meegs/Mono/Uncle Claw—the best SuperBrother I know—F.W.D.

Clarion Books, 215 Park Avenue South, New York, NY 10003 • Text copyright © 2009 by Beth Cadena • Illustrations copyright © 2009 by Frank W. Dormer • The illustrations were executed in Winsor & Newton Artist's Watercolor. • The text was set in 24-point Triplex Serif Light. • All rights reserved. • For information about permission to reproduce selections from this book, write to Permissions, Houghton Mifflin Harcourt Publishing Company, 215 Park Avenue South, New York, NY 10003. • Clarion Books is an imprint of Houghton Mifflin Harcourt Publishing Company. • www.clarionbooks.com • Printed in Singapore • *Library of Congress Cataloging-in-Publication Data* • Cadena, Beth, Supersister / by Beth Cadena ; illustrated by Frank W. Dormer. • p. cm. • Summary: A young girl does all kinds of things around the house to help her pregnant mother, proud that when the new baby comes she is going to be "a super sister." • ISBN: 978-0-547-01006-9 • [1. Helpfulness—Fiction.] I. Dormer, Frank W., ill. II. Title. • PZ7.C11712 Su 2009 [E]—22 2008011618 • TWP 10 9 8 7 6 5 4 3 2 1

by BETH CADENA

Illustrated by FRANK W. DORMER

Clarion Books
Houghton Mifflin Harcourt
Boston   New York
2009

Supersister bounds out of bed. Another super day.

Hark! A call from the kitchen. Mother is in need.

Supersister dashes down the stairs

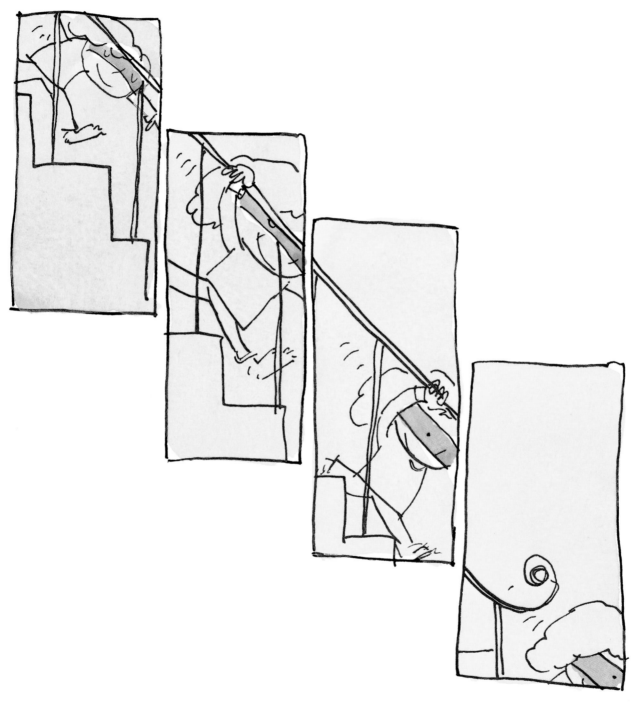

like a whistling locomotive.

She rescues the cereal box from Mother's weary hand. This is a job for Supersister.

She pours!

She spoons!

She spills—

a little.

It's time for school. Backpacked and buttoned, Supersister is determined to strike out for the bus stop alone.

She looks back only twice.

(Even Supersister likes to know Mother is watching.)

Wait! Supersister has forgotten two things.

She races home for a kiss and to tie Mother's shoes.

At school, Supersister dots all of her i's. She crosses all of her t's. She thinks up three new ways to help Mother.

"Super work,"
says her teacher.

The class heads outside for recess.

Supersister is super pleased with herself.

She slides like a speeding bullet. *Wheee!*
Swings like a shooting rocket. *Whoosh!*

Hangs like a mighty monkey. *Ee-ee-ee!*

After school, Supersister springs into action.

First, she takes her dog, Poopsie, for a walk.
Supersister is a super dog walker.

She runs! She skips! She scoops!

She doesn't step in anything. Almost.

Next, she sets the table for dinner.

Supersister is a super setter. Plates. Cups. Forks.

She doesn't drop a thing.

After dinner, she reads a story to Poopsie.

Supersister is a super reader.

She reads the story thirteen times.

Super loud.

Supersister has been a super helper. She'll
think up more ways to help Mother tomorrow.

Now it's time for bed.

Of course Supersister tucks herself in.

She calls out only six times.

Make that seven.

(Even Supersister likes to know Mother is listening.)

Supersister counts sheep to fall asleep.
One sheep, two sheep . . .

. . . ten sheep.   Wait!

Supersister has forgotten two things.

She hurries downstairs for a kiss and to
untie Mother's shoes.

She pats Mother's enormous belly.
"Like I always say, you're going to be a super
sister," says Mother.

"Soon?" asks Supersister.
"Very soon," says Mother.

Supersister bounces back to bed.

She counts just one woolly sheep.

She dreams her super sister dream.

Another super night.